ABOUT THE 2STEVES

Steve Barlow was born in Crewe, in the UK, and has worked at various times as a teacher, an actor, a stage manager and a puppeteer in England, and in Botswana, Africa. He met Steve Skidmore at a school in Nottingham and the 2Steves began writing together. Steve Barlow now lives in Somerset and sails a boat named Which Way, so called because he usually hasn't a clue where he's going.

Steve Skidmore is shorter and less hairy than Steve Barlow. After passing some exams at school, he went on to Nottingham University where he spent most of his time playing sport and doing a variety of heroic summer jobs, including counting pastry pie lids (honest). He trained as a teacher of Drama, English and Film Studies, before teaming up with Steve Barlow to become a full-time author.

Together they have written many books, including Crime Team and Horror. Find out more at:
www.the2steves.net

ABOUT THE ILLUSTRATOR

Sonia Leong is based in Cambridge, in the UK, and is a super-star manga artist. She won Tokyopop's first UK Rising Stars of Manga competition (2005-06) and her first graphic novel was Manga Shakespeare: Romeo and Juliet. She's a member of Sweatdrop Studios and has too many awards to fit in this teeny space.
Find Sonia at her website: www.fyredrake.net

Also by the 2Steves, published by Hachette Children's Books:

Crime Team –
Skull Island
Tiger's Lair
Russian Gold
City of Terror

iHorror –
Vampire Hunter
Zombie Hunter
Werewolf Hunter
Demon Hunter

I HERO

Castle
of Doom

Steve Barlow and Steve Skidmore
Illustrated by Sonia Leong

EDGE
FRANKLIN WATTS

LONDON•SYDNEY

First published in 2011
by Franklin Watts

Franklin Watts
338 Euston Road
London NW1 3BH

Franklin Watts Australia
Level 17/207 Kent Street
Sydney, NSW 2000

A CIP catalogue record for this book
is available from the British Library.

ISBN: 978 1 4451 0268 9

1 3 5 7 9 10 8 6 4 2

Printed in Great Britain

Franklin Watts is a division of Hachette Children's Books,
an Hachette UK company.
www.hachette.co.uk

Decide your own destiny...

This book is not like others you may have read. You are the hero of this adventure. It is up to you to make decisions that will affect how the adventure unfolds.

Each section of this book is numbered. At the end of most sections, you will have to make a choice. The choice you make will take you to a different section of the book.

Some of your choices will help you to complete the adventure successfully. But choose carefully, some of your decisions could be fatal!

If you fail, then start the adventure again and learn from your mistake.

If you choose correctly you will succeed in your adventure.

Don't be a zero, be a hero!

You are the last of the great warrior wizards, living in a world of magic and monsters. Your skill as a wizard is only matched by your skills in sword fighting. You are known as being both wise and brave.

Many different types of creature live in your world. Goblins, trolls and dwarfs live side by side with men and women. You have spent your life fighting against the forces of darkness and always won… so far.

It is the time of Midwinter and you are at home, eating a hearty supper and reading an old book of spells in front of a roaring fire. As you read of ancient spells to defeat demons there is a loud and desperate knocking at the door. You know at once that someone needs your help…

Now go to section 1.

1

"Door open," you say. The door springs open at your command. A flurry of snow whips into the room. A young man stands in the doorway.

"If you are a friend, then enter," you say. The man staggers in. "My name is Muto. I am a friend and I hope that you will be our friend. There is a great evil rising in the lands of the North. Only you can help us…"

If you wish to make sure that Muto is who he says he is, go to 24.

If you wish to listen to Muto's story, go to 38.

2

"So where are the ropes that bound you?" you say. You quickly hold out your staff. "Show your true self!"

Green flame shoots from your staff and the beautiful woman disappears! In her place stands the true creature – a six-headed hag! It spits venom at you. You dodge the poison and it hits a rock, which starts to dissolve!

To use your sword against the hag, go to 10. If you wish to use magic, go to 35.

3

"I will pay you nothing," you say.

"We'll see about that," growls the larger of the Grobllins. The creatures step forward, weapons raised. Although they are fierce creatures, they are stupid to challenge you. With a sigh, you point your staff at them.

If you wish to kill the Grobllins, go to 47.
If you want to let them live, go to 36.

4

You decide that you will have to attack the Count. Luckily, you have the element of surprise. With lightning speed you draw your sword, leap onto the top table and plunge the blade into Count Doom's chest.

The hall goes silent. The Count looks at you and rises from his chair. He looks at the sword and begins to laugh! "You fool! Have you not heard I am a *heartless* man? I cannot be killed by being stabbed!"

You remember the words spoken in the tavern. "How can that be?" you ask.

"You will never know," replies the Count

as he pulls out the sword from his chest and before you can react, plunges it into your body.

You have failed in your quest. To try again, go back to 1.

5

You realise that it would be foolish to set off on your quest in the dead of night. The news of Count Doom troubles you, so you cast a protecting hex on your house, to keep out any unwanted visitors while you sleep. You pack a bag and head to bed, but you do not get much rest. Your sleep is troubled by dreams of monstrous demons and grotesque creatures.

You rise at dawn, slide your sword into its scabbard, pick up your staff and head out. You look at the snow and see that there are many strange footprints around your home. You were right to put on the hex to keep away these creatures of the night.

You head for the stable, saddle up your horse and take the road north.

Go to 13.

6

You hand over your sword and staff, but you are now defenceless. A goblin steps forward grinning at you. His teeth are black and rotten.

Before you have time to react, he smashes his wooden club onto your head, knocking you senseless. You crash to the ground in a heap.

Go to 42.

7

You walk over to the table. "May I join you?" you ask.

"If you have money to play and are prepared to lose it," replies one of the dwarfs.

You smile, throw a bag of coins on the table, order a drink and join in the game. The cards fall well for you and within half an hour, you have won a large pile of coins. The dwarfs are not happy with you. They look at you in hatred and finger their knives below the table.

If you wish to continue playing, go to 19.

If you want to ask them if they know of Count Doom, go to 22.

8

You tell the old man of your quest to destroy Count Doom.

"Then our meeting was meant," he says. He takes out a small golden key from the leather pouch on his belt. "This is the key to Count Doom's heart."

You look puzzled. "Tell me more."

"Several months ago, a fellow healer was asked to make a potion to help cure a man whose chest had been ripped open. He did so, but he found out more than he should. He discovered that this man was Count Doom and by using the dark arts, he had his heart removed and placed in a golden chest!

"To cut a long tale short, my friend stole the key to the chest. He knew the Count would hunt him down and so he gave the key to me. He was right, the Count did find him, but he died without revealing where the key was. And now, I give you the key to Doom's heart as a gift. Use it well." He holds out the key.

You take it and bid the old man farewell.

Go to 16.

9

You leap towards your sword, but the creature is too quick. It grabs hold of you, digging its claws into your arm. Your flesh is ripped open. You have no time to utter a magic spell as the creature's razor sharp teeth rip into your throat, cutting off your cries forever.

To begin your adventure again, go to 1.

10

You pull out your sword as the hag attacks again. All six heads spit at you and some of the deadly venom hits your body. You cry out in pain as it burns into your skin.

You swing your sword wildly and manage to chop off one of the creature's heads. To your horror, another head immediately grows back and spits more of its poison at you.

If you wish to continue to fight using your sword, go to 44.

If you wish to use magic, go to 35.

11

You urge your horse on. Suddenly it rears up and throws you off. Your staff flies from your hand as you hit the ground with a crunch.

Before you can pick yourself up, several large figures leap at you from out of the trees. Their snarls and howls cut through the forest night. Your blood chills as you realise that your attackers are wolfmen! Their great jaws snap at you, revealing their razor sharp teeth.

To try to find your staff, go to 41.
If you wish to use your sword, go to 26.

12

"I have news for your master," you tell the ogre.
"I must see him now."

The ogre picks his nose thoughtfully.
The other guards stare at you and ready
their weapons. The devil dogs spit fire on
the ground.

The ogre finally speaks. "All right, follow me.
But first give me your sword and staff."

If you wish to do as the ogre says, go to 6.

If you wish to fight your way in, go to 23.

**If you wish to use magic to gain entry, go
to 39.**

13

You ride for many hours across the snow-filled
landscape. Morning turns to afternoon and
soon the winter sun begins to set. You arrive
at a crossroads. You wonder which path you
should take.

If you wish to take the forest road, go to 28.

If you wish to take the river road, go to 43.

If you wish to head to the tavern, go to 34.

14

You move slowly towards the Count.

But before you can draw your sword, the Count points at you. "Welcome to my feast, hero." He smiles an evil smile. It is as if he knew you were here.

If you want to rush at him with your sword, go to 30.

If you wish to use magic to fight him, go to 20.

15

You head to the bar. "I need a bed for the night."

The tavern keeper nods. "We have a room available. But first tell me, who are you and what brings you here?"

You tell him your name and your quest. The tavern goes quiet. One of the goblin customers stares at you.

"Your name is known in these parts," the tavern keeper says. "We are honoured to have you as our guest." He hands you a free drink. "Count Doom is known also – he is an evil man. They say he is heartless and cannot be killed as a human can."

As you talk to the keeper about Count Doom, you see the goblin sneaking out of the tavern.

If you wish to follow the goblin, go to 33.
If you wish to head to your room, go to 48.

16

You leave the old man and continue your journey northwards.

After another day of travelling, you finally reach the great mountains and see your destination – the castle of Count Doom! You carefully make your way to the castle.

As you head towards the stone bridge that leads to the castle, your horse refuses to go any further. You dismount and make your way to the castle entrance. Ogres, goblins and two rock giants guard the gate. Devil dogs strain at their leashes as you approach.

One of the ogres steps forward. "Who are you and what do you want?" it grunts.

If you wish to talk your way into the castle, go to 12.

If you wish to fight your way in, go to 23.

If you wish to use magic to gain entry, go to 39.

17

You are too quick for the creature. With a great leap, you fly over the creature's head and reach out for your wizard's staff. You spin around and point it at the creature.

"Be still!" you cry. A blinding sheet of flame leaps from your staff and envelops the creature in a net of fire. The Mutator snarls at you in hatred, and utters foul oaths and curses. But it can do nothing – you have complete power over the creature.

If you wish to kill the creature, go to 45.
If you wish to question it, go to 31.

18

You head over to the Great Hall. A rock giant wearing black chainmail and holding a huge broadsword blocks your way. "Where do you think you are going without any food for the Eve-of-War feast?" he growls.

You realise that it would be foolish to fight the guard with so many soldiers about.

If you wish to use magic on the guard, go to 37.

If you wish to head back to the kitchens, go to 27.

19

As you pick up the cards to deal, one of the dwarfs pulls out his dagger. "To win so much so quickly means that you are cheating…" he says. "We don't like cheats, do we, lads?"

The others nod and pull out their knives. The tavern goes quiet.

If you wish to fight, go to 30.

If you wish to explain who you are, go to 22.

20

You leap onto a table and hold out your staff.
"Meet your doom!"

The hall goes quiet. All eyes stare at you.
Count Doom stares at you.

"Begone!" you command. Nothing happens.
You glare at your staff in shock.

"I knew you would pay me a visit," laughs the
Count. "That's why I put on a protecting hex –
no one can use magic in this castle, except me!"
He holds out his staff and a powerful bolt of
lightning shoots from it. It hits you in the chest
and you crash to the floor, senseless.

Go to 42.

21

"What will it cost?" you ask.

"Your life," roars the Grobllin as it springs
forward, swinging its axe.

You point your staff at your attacker. A finger
of flame bursts from the staff and the axe drops
from the Grobllin's hand. The creature drops to

the floor, stunned. The other Grobllin stands at the bridge looking puzzled.

If you wish to kill the Grobllins, go to 47.
If you want to let them live, go to 36.

22

"I only play for amusement," you say. "This money means nothing to me. Have it back."

The players look at you in astonishment. "In return, I ask one thing. Do you know of Count Doom?"

One of the dwarfs nods. "I have recently returned from the Northern lands. The tales of the Count are growing. They say he is powerful and cannot be killed in combat by magic or blade. They say he is a heartless man. That is all I know."

He sounds like a powerful foe, you think. "Thank you for your information," you say.

If you wish to keep your winnings, go to 30.
If you wish to talk to the tavern keeper, go to 15.

23

"I wish to see your master, and you will not stop me," you say as you draw your sword. With a quick swing, you remove the ogre's head from his body.

The other guards attack. The devil dogs leap at you, breathing fire. You roll out of the way and despatch the creatures with several lightning fast blows.

However, there are too many guards for you to deal with. The rock giants step forward and blast you with two shockwaves. You collapse, dropping your sword and staff. Seeing that you are defenceless, a goblin rushes at you with its jagged teeth bared…

Go to 9.

24

In one movement, you pick up your wizard's staff and point it at Muto. "Show your true self," you order. Muto leaps towards you, but he is too slow. A sheet of green flame bursts from the staff and envelops the man. There is a growling and roaring noise as Muto begins to transform into a foul demon. Muto is really a Mutator – a shape-changer!

The creature snarls at you in hatred and utters foul oaths and curses. But it can do nothing – you have complete power over it. You wonder why it is here.

If you wish to kill the creature, go to 45.
If you wish to question it, go to 31.

25

You hurry over to the old man. He is struggling as you untie his gag.

"It's a trap!" cries the old man. You turn and see that the girl has vanished! In her place stands a nightmarish sight – a six-headed hag! The creature spits venom at you. You dodge the poison and it hits a rock, which starts to dissolve!

To use magic on the hag, go to 35.
To fight the hag with your sword, go to 10.

26

As you pull out your sword, you shout out "Light!" On the ground, your wizard's staff beams out a brilliant white glow, lighting up the darkness.

Your three attackers are taken by surprise. They are momentarily blinded and you take advantage. A quick chop and thrust with your blade takes out one of the wolfmen.

The other two creatures leap at you, but your fighting skills are too good for these beasts. You spin away and your sword hums through the air. Another of your enemies falls to the ground, dead.

The third creature holds back, but you are in no mood for showing mercy. You launch into a devastating attack and your sword bites into the wolfman's flesh. It howls in pain and falls to the ground.

You pick up your staff and calm down your horse. You decide that it would be best to head back to the tavern for a night's rest.

Go to 34.

27

You head into the kitchens. It is hot with the heat of roaring fires. Dwarf cooks are shouting orders. "Get this food to the hall for the Eve-of-War feast!" One of the cooks points at you. "Take in these roast birds. Hurry up!"

You pick up the platter of food and head towards the hall with the other servants. You pass by the giant guard and into the hall, which is loud with the sound of feasting.

You put the platter on a table and look around. Creatures of all kinds are sitting down stuffing their faces. Sitting on the top table is a man with long silver hair – you know at once that this is Count Doom.

If you wish to attack Count Doom using magic, go to 20.

If you wish to use your sword, go to 14.

If you wish to wait to see what happens, go to 46.

28

You urge your horse along the forest path. It gets darker and the path becomes narrower.

Your horse slows down. It is scared. You bring it to a halt and peer into the gloom of the trees. You light your staff, but can see nothing. The only sound you can make out is the breathing of your horse.

If you wish to head back to the tavern for the night, go to 34.

If you wish to continue along the path, go to 11.

29

You shake your head. "I have no time to spare, I must go. Count Doom awaits me."

The old man's eyes open wide. "I know of Count Doom!"

If you wish to tell him of your quest, go to 8.

If you wish to leave the old man, go to 16.

30

Before you can move, you feel a hard blow to the back of your head. Someone, or something, has crept up behind you.

You stagger. You see a blade heading for your throat. You feel a searing pain and your lifeblood gushes out.

If you wish to begin your adventure again, go to 1.

31

"Who sent you, demon?" you command. "And why?"

The creature is in your power and has to answer you. "My master is Count Doom," it snarls. "His name is also doom for you. His power grows. His goal is to be the master of all the lands of the world. He prepares for war and believes that only you have the power to stop him and so you must die."

"Where does this Count live?"

"In his great castle, in the lands of the North."

You have heard all you need. "Enough! Begone, demon!" you cry. The flame that surrounds the creature flares bright red and in an instant, the Mutator is reduced to ashes. At your command, the ashes form into a black cloud and swirl up and out of the chimney.

"So, Count Doom," you mutter. "I think I should pay you a visit and deal with you."

If you wish to set off for Castle Doom immediately, go to 49.

If you wish to wait until morning, go to 5.

32

You remember the old man's words, and reach into your pocket for the golden key.

You move slowly towards the golden chest, but as you do Count Doom suddenly rises from his chair. "I wondered when you would join us," he says. "Welcome to your doom!"

He holds up a staff and a bolt of green flame shoots from it. You leap to the side, just managing to avoid the deadly attack.

To use magic against the Count, go to 20.

To attack the Count with your sword, go to 30.

To break the glass cabinet, go to 50.

33

"Excuse me," you say to the tavern keeper. You pick up your staff, pull your sword from its scabbard and follow the goblin outside into the darkness.

"Light," you command and your staff brightens up the darkness. However, there is no sign of the goblin. As you look around, you give a cry of horror; your horse lies bleeding on the straw-covered ground.

As you kneel down beside the poor creature, you feel a blow to the back of your head. Stunned, you turn and look up into the evil face of the goblin. He smashes the sword and staff from your hands.

"Greetings from my master," it hisses into your face.

Go to 9.

34

You take the road to the Dancing Frog tavern, and soon reach it. There is noise coming from inside the building, so you tie up your horse and enter.

You step into the smoke-filled room. The noise stops as the locals turn and stare at you.

You nod at them and they resume their conversations. You look around, wondering if anyone has information about Count Doom.

If you wish to talk to a group of dwarfs who are playing cards, go to 7.

If you wish to talk to the tavern keeper, go to 15.

35

Before the hag can resume the attack, you hold out your staff. "Begone, hag!" you command.

A white flame shoots from your staff and explodes. You close your eyes as an intense light fills the air and the ground shakes. When you open your eyes, the creature is no more.

You hurry over to the old man and untie his bonds.

"Thank you," he says. "You have saved my life!"

"Tell me how you came to be here," you say.

"I am a maker of potions and cures. I travel the country, collecting herbs and plants for my medicines. This morning I arrived here to pick water flowers, and that is when I was captured by the hag. You arrived just in time. But what brings you here?" he asks.

If you wish to tell the man about your quest, go to 8.

If you wish to get on with your quest, go to 29.

36

"You are lucky I am in a merciful mood," you tell the Grobllins as you urge your horse forward to cross the bridge.

However, being thankful is not in the nature of Grobllins, and your horse is brought down with a terrible blow from a Grobllin club. You crash to the ground. Your staff spins from your grip and drops over the edge of the bridge.

You stagger to your feet and draw your sword. You manage to kill one of the Grobllins with a simple thrust of your sword, but the other one smashes his spiked club into your back. You drop your sword. It lies on the ground as the Grobllin moves in for the kill.

Go to 9.

37

You hold out your staff. "You will let me pass," you command.

Nothing happens.

The rock giant laughs. "So you're a wizard, are you? Count Doom said we might have visitors, so he's put on a protection hex. No one can use magic inside this castle!"

You turn to run, but the rock giant's fist smashes down onto your head.

Go to 42.

38

"Tell me your story," you tell Muto.

"Could I first have a warming drink?" he asks. "I have travelled far and the night is cold…"

"Of course," you say and turn to reach for a flagon of wine that is warming in front of the fire. But as you turn your back, you hear a growling noise. You spin around to see that Muto has disappeared. In his place stands a foul demon. You realise that Muto is really a Mutator – a shape-changer! With an inhuman cry, the creature springs at you.

If you wish to try to reach for your wizard's staff, go to 17.

If you want to try to reach your sword, go to 9.

39

"You will let me pass," you say. Your staff sends out a beam of light, which turns all the guards into living statues. They can only stare at you as you walk past them and into the castle courtyard.

The courtyard is a hive of activity. Creatures of all shapes and sizes are sharpening weapons and loading provisions onto carts. You realise that Count Doom is preparing for war! The creatures do not bother you – they think that you are another of Count Doom's followers.

You look around the courtyard. To the right of you are the kitchens and ahead of you is a great hall.

If you wish to head to the Great Hall, go to 18.

If you wish to head to the kitchens, go to 27.

40

You travel for two days, stopping only to eat
and to allow your horse to rest. The Northern
mountains are now within view. You pass
through many villages, but see no one.

On the following day you are travelling
through a gorge, when you hear muffled cries
for help. You spur on your horse and come to a
waterfall where you see a young woman and an
old man.

The old man is tied up and gagged. "Help
me!" cries the woman. "We have been captured.

Our attackers left us here, but they will be returning soon!"

"Why are you not bound?" you ask the girl.

"I untied myself," she replies. "Please help!"

If you want to do as the woman asks, go to 25.
If you want to question the woman, go to 2.

41

You scramble desperately for your staff as the wolfmen continue their attack.

"Light," you cry, but it is too late! One of the beasts smashes into you and clamps its teeth around your throat, snapping your neck.

You are dead. To begin again, go to 1.

42

Hours later, you wake up chained to the wall of a damp cellar. A goblin stands in front of you.

"Finally awake, are you? Good. The master said that you should feel the pain of dying." He moves forward, holding a red-hot blade. Fortunately, you do not feel pain for long.

You have failed. To begin again, go to 1.

43

You urge your horse down the road towards the river. It grows darker and you hold up your staff to light up the way. After an hour of travelling, you arrive at a wooden bridge, spanning a great river.

From the light of your staff you see that there are two large figures blocking your way. They are armed with axes and spiked wooden clubs.

"Grobllins," you mutter to yourself. Grobllins are a cross between a troll and a goblin. They are dangerous creatures.

The uglier of the two steps forward and growls. "You must pay to cross the bridge."

If you wish to pay, go to 21.
If don't wish to pay, go to 3.

44

Once again, you swing your sword at your enemy. The hag avoids your attack and all of its six heads spit at you. You cannot avoid the deadly stream of venom.

The poison hits your eyes and you scream in agony. Blinded, you drop your sword and rub at your face. You are unable to see as the hag moves in for the kill. You fumble for your staff, but it is hopeless. The creature's heads spit at you, time after time, burning and dissolving your body until you finally sink into the welcome release of death.

You have failed in your quest. If you wish to begin again, go to 1.

45

Begone, foul demon!" you cry. The flame that surrounds the creature flares bright red and in an instant, the Mutator is reduced to ashes.

"Return to the air," you command. The creature's ashes form into a black cloud and swirl up and out of the chimney.

You wonder who sent the creature, but because you have destroyed it you will never know. You return to your chair to read your book of spells.

Your adventure is over before it began. To start again, return to 1.

46

As the feast continues you look around the hall. Ogres, goblins and giants sit discussing their plans for waging war. You know that the lands of the world would be ravaged by such an alliance of peoples.

You wonder what you should do. Again you look around the hall. Behind the top table, you see a glass cabinet. In it stands a golden chest.

If the old man you saved gave you a gift,
go to 32.

If he didn't, and you wish to attack the
Count using magic, go to 20.

If he didn't and you wish to attack the
Count with your sword, go to 4.

47

You know that you cannot let such creatures live – if you do, they will surely take the lives of innocent travellers.

You hold out your staff. "Begone!" A swirl of flame shoots out and in an instant, the evil creatures are nothing more than a pile of ash.

By now it is very dark. You peer across the bridge and make out the outlines of tall trees. Who knows what creatures may be lurking there? You have travelled far today and must now make a decision.

If you wish to head back to the Dancing Frog tavern, go to 34.

If you wish to continue into the forest, go to 28.

48

You realise that there is little point in following the goblin – word of your quest will already have got back to Count Doom.

You ask the tavern keeper to make sure that your horse is stabled and then head for your room. You cast a protection hex on the room and have a good night's sleep.

You rise early in the morning, have breakfast and are soon back on the road, heading north for your battle with Count Doom.

Go to 40.

49

Despite the late hour, you gather together a travelling bag, slide your sword into its scabbard, pick up your staff and open the door. As you step out into the winter night, you suddenly feel a sense of unease.

"Light," you command. Your staff glows, lighting up the darkness and revealing a terrible sight. Dozens of grotesque creatures are standing in front of you, snarling and grunting. Before you can react, the creatures spring at you, knocking your staff from your hand.

You try to fight back, but there are too many of them. Their claws and teeth rip at your flesh and your blood pumps from your body, staining the white winter snow.

If you wish to begin your adventure again, turn back to 1.

50

More bolts of flame shoot from the Count's staff, but you manage to avoid them.

You run and somersault over Count Doom, cracking him on the head with your staff as you fly. You smash into the glass cabinet and quickly pick up the chest. You unlock it. Inside, lying on a red silk scarf, is a beating heart!

You place the point of your sword against it. "No!" screams the Count, his face filled with horror. "Please? I will give you anything. Perhaps you want gold? Or to rule the world with me?"

"I am not for sale," you reply. You thrust your blade into the heart. Count Doom falls to the ground clutching at his breast. You twist the blade, and he roars in pain.

There is a deafening explosion of light and heat as the Count and all his followers are reduced to ash and smoke. And then there is quiet.

You look around. You have defeated Count Doom and his followers. Your world is safe. You are a true hero!

ARTIST AT WORK!

Hi there! I'm Sonia, and I draw all the artwork in the I HERO books. I work mainly as a manga artist and I run drawing workshops, too.

I draw in three main stages for I HERO. First, I sketch out the rough positions in pencil. Then I make any changes and work up the art in ink. Finally, I add layers of texture for the fills and shadows.

This piece from paragraph 24 shows how important it is to balance your shading. I've created a dark outer circle and a lighter inner frame to highlight the darker skin of the shape-changer.

I HERO FAN ART

These pieces were sent in
by R. Logan from Queen
Elizabeth's in Devon.
Steve Skidmore said:
"It's us – but obviously
we have more muscles!"

Want the chance to see *your* I HERO fan art*
in an I HERO book? Send it to:

I HERO fan art
EDGE/Franklin Watts
15th Floor, 338 Euston Road, London NW1 3BH

or email it to:

ad@hachettechildrens.co.uk

*Sorry, but we won't be able to return any art to you – so take a photo of it first!
Write your name, age and address on each piece of fan art.

Alien Raid

Steve Barlow and Steve Skidmore
Illustrated by Sonia Leong

It is the year 2150. You are a top Flight Commander in the Galaxy Defence Force (GDF). You have taken part in hundreds of dangerous missions for the GDF. You have also fought in many battles against hostile alien life forms, who wish to conquer Earth.

You and your Flight Squadron are based on the GDF base on the planet Mars. It is Earth's forward defence against any alien attacks.

You are asleep in your dorm pod, when you are awoken by an alarm. A computer voice screams out. "Code Alpha Alert!"

You snap awake. Code Alpha is the alert signal for an alien attack!

**Continue reading the adventure in
I HERO Alien Raid**

DECIDE YOUR
OWN DESTINY

I HERO

EDGE

Alien Raid

Steve Barlow - Steve Skidmore

Want to read more "You Are The Hero" adventures? Well, why not try these...

Also by the 2Steves: iHorror
Fight your fear. Choose your fate.

978 1 40830 985 8 pb
978 1 40831 476 0 eBook

978 1 40830 986 5 pb
978 1 40831 477 7 eBook

978 1 40830 988 9 pb
978 1 40831 479 1 eBook

978 1 40830 987 2 pb
978 1 40831 478 4 eBook